For Oscar

Not Without My Whale

By Billy Coughlan   Illustrated by Villie Karabatzia

"I'm not going," Arnold sniffed.

"I'm not going," Arnold cried.

"I'm not going," Arnold wept.

"I am NOT going," Arnold sobbed.

"Not without my whale!"

"It's **too big**," said Uncle Bob.

"And pooh!!! It's far **too smelly**," said Grandma, holding her nose.

"**I think we can manage**," said Dora from next door with a skipping rope in one hand, a watering can in the other and a skateboard under her arm.

Arnold and his whale went to school.

"You can't bring that whale into assembly," Mrs Oates said. "It's *too noisy*."

Arnold hung his head. He could never remember the hymns.

"Then I'm not singing," he whispered.

"Not without my whale."

She waved her baton in the air.
Arnold and his whale and all the
children sang beautifully.

"You can't bring that whale into maths,"
said Mrs Oates. "It's too wet."

Arnold's lip began to wobble.

He always got in a muddle with sums.

"Then I'm not coming," he said.
"Not without my whale."

"I think we can manage," said Dora.

She pointed to the benches outside and
handed out umbrellas and wellington boots.

The class sat in the playground and counted bubbles.

"You can't bring that whale to football practice," said Mrs Oates. "It's too big."

Arnold looked down at his boots. Nobody ever picked him for their team.

"Then I'm not playing," he mumbled. "Not without my whale."

"I think we can manage," said Dora
with a whistle between her teeth.

Nobody could kick the ball past Arnold's whale and his enormous tail was fantastic for flicking it down the other end of the pitch.

Arnold and the whale's team won the game 37 - 0.

At lunchtime everyone talked to Arnold. They took turns feeding his whale fish from a bucket.

At first Arnold was shy, but he soon
began to chat with his new friends.

In fact they all had so much fun they didn't hear the bell. They didn't line up. Mrs Oates tapped her foot angrily.

"I am very disappointed," she said. "You will all stay in for extra sums at afternoon break!"

"And Arnold, your whale can do sums too!"

Arnold looked at the empty fish bucket.

He caught the fishiest whiff of what was to come.

Dora winked and handed him a peg.

Arnold grinned.

"I think we can manage," he said.

The End

No Without My Whale
An original concept by author Billy Coughlan
© Billy Coughlan
Illustrations by Villie Karabatzia

Published by MAVERICK ARTS PUBLISHING LTD
Studio 3A, City Business Centre, 6 Brighton Road,
Horsham, West Sussex, RH13 5BB
© Maverick Arts Publishing Limited September 2015 +44 (0)1403 256941

A CIP catalogue record for this book is available at the British Library.

ISBN 978-1-84886-182-4

Maverick
arts publishing

www.maverickbooks.co.uk